I0571147

THE GOLDEN ARROW
AND OTHER TALES

The Golden Arrow

Arrow

and Other Tales

written & illustrated by

SAMANTHA GILLOGLY

Artistic Media Associates, Inc.
www.artisticmediaassociates.com

FIRST EDITION

Front cover stock photograph by LyG-photo
Cover design by Samantha Gillogly

ISBN-10: 0986434507
ISBN-13: 978-0-9864345-0-1

CONTENTS

1

A GARLAND AS LONG AS THE YEAR

The princess had sight, but she had no eyes. Where her eyes should have been, there were two azure flowers. Each day, these flowers opened to greet the dawn, their petals unfurling as blue and unclouded as the sky itself. Each night, they folded like hands in prayer as the princess slept in her high, windy tower.

"Unnatural!"

"A curse!"

"No man will wed that."

The day the princess was born, her eyes had hardly bloomed for the first time when the king's court declared she was unfit to show her face in public. Many thought her strangeness was the work of witchcraft. Some said it would be a sin to let her live.

But the queen's midwife loved the child instantly. She begged the king and queen to let her care for the little girl with the flower eyes. "I will shield her from those who would wish her ill," said the midwife. "She will be safely hidden, and your Majesties will not be disgraced."

And so for many years, the midwife and the princess dwelt together in the highest tower in the castle. Their chamber was so remote that the trill of birdsong could be heard more often than the chatter of daily castle life.

To pass the days, the midwife spun thread with her fingers, and spun stories with her words. The princess watched and listened with rapt attention. She learned the art of twisting raw wool into yarn, and raw words into tapestries of tales. It was a quiet existence, but not altogether lonely. So long as she and the midwife were together, as close and comfortable as two twining threads, the princess would be contented.

One cold winter morning—the dawn of the princess' 17th birthday—a plague descended upon the land. It came on haunted, hungry wings, slowly picking off townsfolk one by one. Grown men were not spared, nor women and children. Young and old alike were stricken dead. The tolling of funeral bells competed with the crackling of bonfires lit to burn away the black sickness. But there was little the people could do to halt the steady march of death. When they were not coughing and croaking with poisoned lungs, they were too weak to even wail in despair.

For a time, the king's castle was safe. But soon even that stronghold was infiltrated. The plague's foul miasma crept through windows and oozed between mossy bricks. First the servants, then the knights and ladies, and finally the royal couple themselves—all were taken ill. Not a single physician in all the kingdom had a tenth the skill it would take to treat their plague-wracked bodies. But the king and queen knew of one person who was wise in many long-forgotten healing arts; one who dwelt within the castle but had not yet fallen prey to the plague; one who might know a cure.

"Do not leave the tower unless I tell you to," warned the

midwife. She grasped the princess' soft white hands in her gnarled calloused ones.

A tiny dew-drop spilled from a blue petal onto the princess' cheek. "I promise," she murmured.

The princess passed the day alone pacing the small tower chamber. She glanced at the door often, never daring to leave the room.

Another day passed. Soon, it had been a week; then, two weeks. The princess began to run out of food. For a distraction, she busied herself spinning wool into yarn. When there was no more wool, she twisted straw. When there was no more straw, she twisted strands of her own hair. Her stomach twisted in hunger. Her hands twisted in silent anguish.

At the end of three weeks, she lay down upon the cold stone floor and wept. She wept until her upturned face was like a pool upon which floated two blue lilies.

Suddenly, there came a fluttering of wings. The princess looked up. A small brown sparrow alighted on her windowsill.

The sparrow tilted its head. It looked the princess up and down with glossy black eyes. Then, it spoke—not in a chirp, but in the midwife's warm, soothing tone: "Thank heaven, child, you're still alive!"

The princess crawled on her hands and knees to the

window. "Can it be?" she gasped. "Is it you? Truly?"

"It is," said the sparrow. "Alas, dear girl, your father the king is dead. It took all my arts to keep your mother alive. In the end, Death took my life as payment for sparing hers. But she may not last much longer. She is very weak. She has but a few servants left to care for her, and they are sick too. Everyone in the kingdom who still clings to life has either fled or will soon take ill. Everyone, that is, except you. Here in the tower, in the pure clean air, you remain untouched by the plague. You are the only soul hale enough to save the queen. Sweet child, I have come to ask you one last favor: you must leave the castle."

"Leave the castle?" said the princess. "But I cannot! To leave the castle, I must walk down every staircase and corridor, every gallery and gate. Surely, along the way, I will be seized by the sickness?"

"Did I say 'walk'?" said the sparrow. Its ruffled feathers hinted at a smile. "Child, there are other ways of moving through this world."

With that, the sparrow hopped off the windowsill and flew away.

"Wait!" the princess cried out. "Come back! Please, do not leave me again! What must I do?"

Her question was met with silence.

Then came a sound like a gale blowing through treetops. Hundreds upon hundreds of sparrows squeezed through the window in a tumult of wings. The flock swooped round the chamber and grabbed up skeins of yarn from the floor. Dashing and diving, the birds wove a web around the princess' wrists and ankles.

As quickly as it had arrived, the flock ceased its frantic flying. Each sparrow took hold of a strand in its beak or toes and nestled quietly among the rafters.

"We are ready," said the midwife, perching upon the princess' shoulder. "Are you?"

The princess understood now. "I am," she said. She held her breath and budded her flower eyes as tight as could be.

Out upon the clear cold air, the sparrows held the princess fast in their web of yarn. They soared through cool mists and playful winds. The princess' hair floated like a cloud of gold, and her gown was as a billowing sail.

Slowly, she opened her blue-petaled eyes. Far below her lay her father's kingdom, an ashen stain of sorrow upon the land. In the distance, a lone bell tolled.

Beyond the walls of the kingdom, fields and forests stretched on forever. The first fragile breath of spring tinged the woods with palest green.

The princess' flower-eyes widened with fear. They budded tight again with sorrow, and wept in wonder.

The birds brought her down to rest upon a hillside of soft new grass. Releasing their strands, the flock disappeared into the sky.

"Wait!" cried the princess, clutching at the air. "What must I do now?"

The midwife's voice sounded from all around her. "You must weave a garland as long as the year," the voice said. "Circle it round the kingdom's bounds. When the end meets the beginning, the queen will be saved, and the kingdom restored."

At last, the princess was alone again.

The air was sharp and chill. To stand still would mean succumbing to the cold.

All day, the princess wandered the empty meadows. She searched for no one and sought nothing. Her only thought was to keep moving and place one foot before the other. She walked and walked, traipsing over hill and valley.

At last she reached a knoll topped by a gnarled, barren tree. The princess paused beneath the tree to lean against it and catch her breath. As she did so, she spied the outer walls of the kingdom far below. Beyond those walls rose the shadowy grey heights of the castle. Somewhere in that castle, her mother the queen still languished in sickness.

The princess sat down. She was too tired to cry anymore.

From the corner of her sight, she noticed a single cord of ivy coiled round the tree trunk. The ivy trailed into a small tendril that tightly grasped the stem of a crisp, white snowdrop.

The princess stared in awe. She had never seen anything so beautiful in all her life. She lay down next to the snowdrop. She hardly blinked her own blue petals lest the white ones shivering before her fade away.

She lay there until weariness overtook her. Then she passed into a sleep as deep as the starry night above.

The princess awoke the next morning, pale and rigid and half-delirious with cold. All around her, the hillside was covered in snowdrops. Like a gathering of white-winged, green-tipped moths, the flowers fluttered and danced in the early dawn breeze.

The princess stiffly reached out and plucked a snowdrop. She held it to her face. Somewhere in the cold, heavy depths of her mind, a memory flickered. It stirred some warmth into her leaden limbs:

"Weave a garland as long as the year…"

The princess sat up and knelt beside the tree. She picked another snowdrop, and another, and another, until her arms were full. Then, beginning with the first ivy-twined blossom, she knotted together flower after flower. When she was finished, she had a chain of snowdrops that was as long as she was tall.

From that day on, the princess wandered the countryside, gathering whatever flowers, fruit, and foliage the earth had to offer. She wove her findings into a single continuous garland. The garland trailed behind her, growing longer and longer with each passing day.

With the spring thaw, snowdrops gave way to purple crocuses and golden daffodils. Bluebells carpeted the forest floor in a faery mist. Apple trees and hawthorns bloomed in a profusion of pink and white. Lily-of-the-valley chimed its fragrant bells in tune with the robin's song. The princess drank the morning dew that shimmered upon the grass, and ate the tender new ferns that uncoiled along the riverbanks.

Leaves grew thicker. Grass grew taller. Callow spring matured to hearty summer. For her garland, the princess gathered leathery oak leaves. She picked acorns, still small and green. There was frothy white elderflower, and yarrow

9

like foam on a wave. There were cowslips bright as butter, and buttercups bright as the sun. Poppies bled through shaggy ears of green-gold grain. The princess ate berries of the forest. Some were bitter, some were sweet, and some were both at once. Haystacks served as her bed. The song of the wind soughing through the wheat fields became her lullaby.

Autumn took its slow turn. The woods and fields exhaled into a brilliant heraldry of color. The princess' garland blazed with leaves of every shade: crimson, scarlet, cherry, rose, salmon, amber, pumpkin, rust, gold, bronze, and feverish flames of sunset. Meadows offered yellow goldenrod and purple daisy. Hedges bore blushing rosehips and clusters of brown hazelnuts. The princess' hands grew raw and red from her labors. In spite of this pain, she climbed fruit trees to soothe her hunger. She ate as many apples and pears as she could gather into her skirt in a day. Sometimes she fell asleep in the branches.

Soon, autumn's splendor sobered to a dull brown. Days grew dimmer. The ground was rimed with frost. Cold, dirty, ragged, and thin, the princess reaped the hardest and hardiest of nature. Her fingers cracked and bled as she wove the rough raiment of winter into her miles-long garland. Fir needles hung with pinecones as prickly as hedgehog quills. Dark polished holly leaves grew in sharp clusters, their berries showing like drops of blood against the swift-falling snow. Once, a low-slung oak branch granted a single sprig of pearly mistletoe. The princess slept in abandoned animal burrows and ancient hollow trees. She nestled in leaf-mould to keep warm. Sometimes she found nuts on the ground, but not enough to live on. When the hunger became unbearable, the princess disguised herself as a blind beggar woman and shielded her flower-eyes with her hair like a veil. Arrayed in this fashion, she supped on the bread-crusts, wine, and firelight of generous traveling strangers.

Winter was long, but the garland never withered. Each leaf and blossom remained as fresh as the day it was plucked. The princess, blue with cold, unyielding as ice, marched onward, trailing the garland behind her. She plaited dry reeds and twigs when there was nothing else to be found.

At last, a day came when winter's grip loosened just a little. The snow ebbed, and the ground softened.

Wandering an open meadow, the princess climbed to the top of a knoll. Crowning the knoll was a single twisted tree. Around this tree spiraled vines of ivy. And from this ivy proceeded a chain of flowers that linked endlessly on and on into the distance. Beyond the knoll and down the valley lay the walls of the kingdom, and above that, the castle.

The princess stood aghast. She had walked, wandered, and woven for a whole year. Without knowing, she had encircled the entire kingdom with her garland.

"*When the end meets the beginning, the queen will be saved, and the kingdom restored...*"

Grasping the end of the garland in her fist, the princess rushed to kneel beneath the tree. She tried to tie the ends together. But her hand stopped short.

By the space of mere inches, the garland was not long enough.

The princess cast about wildly, searching for a leaf, bud, or stem; something, anything with which to complete the garland. But not a single plant, dead or alive, could be found on the bare hillside.

The princess fell to her knees. For the first time in many months, the cold resolve in her heart began to thaw. It flowed up into her head and spilled out as tears upon her wind-raw cheeks.

"Has all my labor, my pilgrimage, been for nothing? Have I failed my one promise, my single purpose?"

She buried her face in her hands. Then she felt the touch of something familiar on her palms: soft petals, blue as cornflower, blue as the sky. Her eyes. Her beautiful, accursed flower-eyes.

The princess realized in an instant what she had to do. She braced herself for the pain to come. Pinching each flower between her fingertips, she gave a mighty pull and plucked her eyes from her face. Hot pain seared through her skull. She collapsed to the ground, sightless and raving. She screamed and sobbed. Then, summoning her last ounce of strength, she recalled to mind the task at hand. With shaking hands she fumbled and grasped for the end of the garland. After a few agonizing seconds, she managed to bind the end of the garland into its beginning using the two brilliant blue flowers.

A wave of warmth washed over her. The pain became only pressure; then the pressure eased away, and she felt nothing—nothing but relief, peace, and the most exquisite joy.

The green, moist warmth of spring filled the air. The princess began to laugh a mad, joyous laugh. She rose to her feet and danced. She spun around and around, exulting in the pure pleasure of being alive. She laughed until her throat could laugh no more. She fell to the ground exhausted, and her soul continued to laugh even as her body slept.

"Incredible!"

"Amazing..."

"By God, it is a miracle."

The princess woke in a daze to the sound of murmuring voices. She was blind, but she knew by touch and smell that she was lying on a real bed, under real linen, next to a warm hearth. She was inside the castle.

Weak but determined, she sat up slowly. "What...what has happened?" she groaned.

The voices around her gasped.

"How did I come here?" she persisted. "Where is my mother the queen?"

A young boy laid his hand on the princess' shoulder. "M'lady, it is so strange a tale, you'd scarce believe it yourself! A flock of birds landed outside and laid your body at the castle gates. One of the guardsmen recognized you from the stories of your... your 'peculiar aspect' is what he called it. He knew you must've been the child of the king and queen. He carried you up to the castle. Everyone in the household—that is, everyone that's left of us—we wanted to come see you for ourselves. And then word got out into the streets that you'd returned. It was nigh impossible to stop all these folk from ambushing the gate to get a look! You see, m'lady... we thought you were dead of the plague a year ago."

The princess' head swam. "And what of my mother?" she asked. "Where is the queen?"

An elder man stepped forward. "My lady, it saddens me to tell you this, but your mother is dead. The sickness was too strong. She relinquished her hold on life some three months back, when winter began to fall."

"This cannot be!" the princess cried. "I was meant to save her! I made a promise to the midwife. I was supposed to save the queen! And now you say she is dead. This cannot be, or else I have truly failed."

"My lady," said the old man, "do not distress yourself with talk of failure! You are weak and famished, and require much rest. Your mother's death dealt a heavy sorrow on us all. And yet, there is now some cause for joy and thanksgiving: for upon the hour of your arrival at the castle gates, men and women on the brink of death arose from their sickbeds in full health. As if by magic, the odorous cloud has lifted. We see the bright sun and the clear blue sky for the first time in over a year. Signs of life are blessedly returning.

"As for the task you speak of: your mother, may her soul rest in heaven, is gone from this world. But by disappearing beyond our plague-ridden kingdom these many months, you have, in a way, 'saved the queen.' For you see, my lady: *you* are now our queen."

Realizing the truth in his words, the princess began to weep silently.

Amidst the flood of tears, she blinked her eyelids. Where her flower-eyes had been, the tears froze in each socket to form two shining orbs of ice.

She blinked again. Now the orbs turned to glass marbles that glistened in the firelight.

She blinked a third time. Now her sight was restored, for now she had eyes; not flower-eyes, but real, true eyes. Eyes as blue as sapphires, eyes as keen as an eagle's, eyes as piercing as a sword. She gazed open-mouthed at the huddled crowd before her. Then she slowly rose from her bed. The hall fell silent. A hundred knees genuflected, and a hundred heads bowed in homage to the princess—the princess who was now queen.

She reigned for many years in peace and plenty. Sickness and want were but a banished memory. She was the finest ruler the kingdom had ever known, and would ever know, for she was blessed with a great gift. She had sight beyond measure. Her eyes could peer leagues into the horizon, and glimpse years into the future. Better than that, they could read the most inscrutable thing of all: the human heart.

In time she learned that to know a heart is to know an entire world. She saw, cloistered within the breasts of her subjects and enemies alike, the darkest pestilence of cruelty or the fairest flower of virtue. Often, both qualities grew in equal measure, intertwining. She who can see this is the wisest person of all, for she perceives the winter and spring in every soul, and embraces them.

2

DRAGONSBLOOD

Three knights of the Black Sash—Sir Alain, Sir Bertran, and Sir Crespin—were returning home from the Crusades. With Palestine far behind them, they were now empty of purse and of stomach. Their lean bellies craved the weight of good white bread. Their weary bodies dreamed of soft white pillows. Their hungry horses longed to crop at sweet grass and walk on beds of straw instead of flinty roads. And yet, to these knights, their rough pilgrimage was a balm compared with the battles they'd left behind—each for his own private reason.

Now, in the sultry dead of summer, the three brethren of the Black Sash neared their destination: the city of Valbrume.

Valbrume was a bustling center of honest trade and hospitality embraced by a valley of white mist. Here the knights hoped they might find peace and a chance to make their fortunes anew.

However, one last trial stood between them and their journey's end.

Jutting from the edge of Valbrume was a mountain. This mountain was topped by a peak so narrow and so sharp, it seemed to pierce Heaven itself. This was the mountain known as *La Corne du Monde*, The Horn of the World.

The knights halted at the foot of the Horn. They gazed up the jagged path that cut back and forth across the mountainside like a scar. The path was littered with yellowed bones. Human skulls grinned from every step.

"That tortuous road will take days to travel!" cried Sir Alain. "Can we not ascend in a straight line?"

"Or avoid climbing all together, and circle round the bottom?" asked Sir Bertran.

"No, brothers," said Sir Crespin. "This mountain is far too steep for our horses to tread off the path. And the slopes on either side are filled with sharp and perilous rocks. It is up the winding road we must journey."

So the knights set off for the long ascent up the sun-bleached Horn of the World.

Three days passed before they reached the peak. The white sun burned their necks, and cold winds lashed their faces. Rounding a corner, they came upon a cave. The mouth of this cave gaped like a ragged wound. A stench belched forth from it, hot and sulfurous. The knights could see nothing in the cave but darkness: blacker than their sashes, blacker than a raven's wing, blacker than all the moonless midnights in the desert.

"Come, let us make camp in here," proclaimed Sir Alain. "It may be odorous, but it will offer some shelter from the sun and wind."

"My heart tells me it is an evil place!" countered Sir Bertran. "Pray, let us venture further and find a more wholesome place to rest."

"Brothers," spoke Sir Crespin, "at this height, there will be few safer spots to make camp; but neither should we tread without caution. Some other wight may call this cave his home. To enter without his leave would be discourteous."

"Discourteous?" scoffed Sir Alain. "What man or

beast could make a home of this savage place and be deserving of our courtesy? Who could reside here already but a heathen wild-man, or the bats who sleep upon the ceiling?"

"What would you have us do, Crespin?" begged Sir Bertran. "Announce ourselves, only to be slain on the threshold by whatever devil lurks within?"

"We cannot fear what we have not yet met," replied Sir Crespin. He stepped forward and cupped his hands to his mouth. "Greetings, master of this hall! We are Sir Alain, Sir Bertran, and Sir Crespin, of the Order of the Black Sash. We are at your service; in return, we beg parlay with you." He bowed low.

"This is folly," growled Sir Alain.

"He is mad!" squealed Sir Bertrand.

A moment later, from the depths of the cave, two glowing yellow orbs appeared—small at first, mere pinpricks of light. They drew closer, growing bigger and bigger, as big as a man's head. Then, they blinked.

Sir Alain drew his sword. Sir Bertran clutched his shield. "Brother, look out!" they cried.

But Sir Crespin remained bowed.

The yellow eyes' smoldering pupils were slit like a serpent's. Shadows fled their piercing stare. Their lamp-like glow revealed a long, spiny visage covered in garnet scales. Wide nostrils puffed plumes of hot smoke.

Sir Alain brandished his sword. Sir Bertran gripped his shield tighter. "Brother, stand back!" they yelled.

But Sir Crespin held his ground.

The scaly head hove forward. Its neck was long, lean, shining, and hard. It coiled against a pair of strong sinuous shoulders. The shoulders stretched into legs, the legs into feet, the feet into toes, and the toes into claws: claws as long as bulls' horns, claws sharper than knives.

Sir Alain charged. Sir Bertrand ducked behind the horses. "Run, Crespin!" they shouted.

But Sir Crespin remained bowed, unmoving.

The dragon emerged fully from the cave. Sun glanced off its scales. The beast spread wide its great webbed wings.

"Out of the way!" cried Sir Alain. He shoved Sir Crespin aside and lunged sword-first at the dragon.

With a single swipe, the dragon knocked the blade from Sir Alain's hand. The sword clattered to the ground as easily as though it were a child's toy.

"*Ssso,*" proclaimed the dragon, its voice like steel rasping against granite, "*knights of the famed Sssash? If this is how you confront your enemiesss, the tales of your ssskill and valor must be very tall indeed.*"

Sir Crespin looked up at last. "Noble wyrm of *La Corne du Monde*, I beg you forgive my fellow knights.

They wish only to protect a brother-in-arms from threats unknown."

"But we know precisely what it is!" cried Sir Alain. "A great, gruesome dragon! An enemy of man, destroyer of cities!"

"And a child of Hell!" gulped Sir Bertran.

The dragon's eyes flashed. Jets of smoke spewed from its nose and mouth. Its dagger-like teeth cut the smoke to grey ribbons.

"*Sssilence! Satan's ssspawn I am not. I shall suffer no such ssslanderous speech! In sooth, I should ssslay you this selfsame second. But,*" it mused, looking thoughtful now, "*I sssuppose some other arrangement could suffice… You vowed your ssservices in exchange for some ssspeech between usss? As you can sssee, I have honored my half of this. So now I beg you sssurrender such servicesss as I ssso require… That is, should you accept the task.*"

"We are knights of the Sash!" declared Sir Alain. "We do not serve monsters."

"Or any force of evil," added Sir Bertran.

"But a true knight does not shrink from a challenge," said Sir Crespin. "What is it you will of us, dragon?"

"*Ssseven long years have I sat atop this ssseat in the sky. Every seven days, I ssswoop down to the city of*

Valbrume and snatch a savory smith, a succulent shepherd, a sssumptuous suzerain, or some other manner of man to sssate my cravings. But such systematic slaughter need not be the sole solution to slake my thirssst. Sssome other sanguinary source can sustain me. Atop this sssummit is a stone sink from which springs a well of blood. I cannot drink ssstraight from it myssself, for the blood flees my tongue and recedesss into the sssoil. Thusss, each day, one of you must fetch a pail of blood from the well and bring it to me for my sssupper. That is my requessst."

"How long are we to do this for?" demanded Sir Alain.

"For ssso long as I am hungry."

"But we ourselves will perish out here in the wilderness with no food or drink!" said Sir Bertran.

"Do not assume I am sssuch an unkind host! You may dwell here in the sssafety of my cave. I shall sssleep out of sssight in the innermost chamber and disturb you not. If each knight is faithful to the tasssk on his appointed day, he will find the mountaintop's trees heavy-laden with fruit. This fruit shall fill your bellies and give ssstrength to sustain you. And from the trees' rootsss shall flow crystal streams of clearest water. This will quench your thirssst and keep your horses hale and full of vigor. I invite you to

eat and drink as much as your need requiresss."

"And what's to prevent us from abandoning this hateful work?" asked Sir Bertran.

"*If you ssso much as attempt to escape ere your service is finished, the path down the mountain will grow thick with briars. The ssstreambeds will run black with poison. You will not last long.*"

"And what if we refuse here and now to partake in any of this?" asked Sir Alain. "We cannot be punished for breaking a vow we have not yet taken."

The dragon nodded ruefully. "*I confesss I cannot bind you to this burden unless you first take it up freely. If you refuse now, no harm shall come to yourselvesss. I shall simply resume feasting upon the folk of Valbrume.*"

Sir Crespin spoke up. "Brothers, do not forget why we set out on this journey. We are Knights of the Sash. We took a solemn oath to protect innocents. We must remain faithful to that pledge, for the safety of Valbrume... and for the sake of our honor."

The knights took turns each day climbing the tip of the Horn to fetch the dragon's supper. Sir Alain went first. He brought with him a silver pail provided by the dragon. Just as the creature had described, Sir Alain found a well carved into a rock ledge. Within the well pooled a spring of blood, fresh as from a man newly-slain. Sir Alain filled the pail until its contents sloshed down the sides and stained his hands red. He carried the bucket back down the path and took it to the dragon's inner chamber in the cave.

"Arise, dragon!" Sir Alain called out, for the beast slept in the daytime and awoke at sundown to dine.

The dragon stirred. It sniffed the bucket and nodded approvingly. *"I shall sssup alone. Go, sir knight, and ssseek your day's reward."*

Sir Alain left the black cave and emerged into the blue twilight. To his astonishment, the dragon's promise held true: trees that were once barren and twisted now burst into leaf anew. Buds blossomed and ripened into golden apples in the blink of an eye. Water clear as crystal gushed from the hollow spaces between roots. Sir Alain plucked an apple from a branch. He devoured one, two, three, and soon seven apples in all. He found a silver cup lying beside the stream and drank greedily of the water. It was cool and sweet and pure. Never had he felt so refreshed, so sated, and so hearty in all his life.

Returning to the cave, he found his fellow knights eating the last of their meager traveling rations. Their horses drank water from a silver trough.

"Brothers, when your turns come, you must eat up!" exclaimed Sir Alain. "These apples and water put strength in the muscle and fortitude in the bones. We cannot afford to be weak while a dragon sleeps next door."

The following day, it was Sir Bertran's turn to traverse the path to the well of blood. He filled the silver pail only halfway. The sight of its gory contents brought more horror on him than all the blood he'd witnessed on the battlefield.

He hurried the bucket back to the cave. In a timid voice he called out, "Arise, dragon!"

The beast awoke, sniffed the pail, and nodded at Sir Bertran. "*I shall sssup alone. Go, sir knight, and ssseek your day's reward.*"

Sir Bertran left the cave. He was met with the same sight Sir Alain beheld the day before: dead trees flush with life, branches laden with gilded fruit, roots unleashing clear water upon the dry streambeds. Sir Bertran plucked a single apple from a tree. He bit into it with caution. Forsaking the silver cup beside the stream, he drank instead but a palmful of water. He swallowed hard.

"Eat what you must to hold off starvation," he said upon returning to camp. "But I fear the effect these bewitched fruits may have over time. I have never beheld their like before! Surely they were not made by the same Hand that shaped the world? We must take care, and never allow them to overpower our bodies or taint our souls."

The day after, Sir Crespin took his turn to fetch the blood from the well. He filled the silver pail as full as he could carry without spilling and brought it to the inner chamber of the cave.

"Arise, dragon!" he called out. He set the pail upon the ground.

The dragon woke, sniffed the pail, and nodded to Sir Crespin. "*I shall sssup alone. Go, sir knight, and ssseek your day's reward.*"

Sir Crespin bowed and thanked the dragon. He left the cave and found the mountainside transformed into a lush orchard laced with shining streams. Sir Crespin picked two apples, but ate only one; the other he stored in a leather pouch. He found the silver cup and drank a few mouthfuls of water before using the rest to wash his hands and face. When he returned to the cave, he offered Sir Bertran the apple he had saved. "Eat this, dear brother. You have grown so pale and feverish since yesterday. I fear you are weak with hunger."

"No," said Sir Bertran, who shivered under his cloak. "Of the serpent's garden I will eat no more! I swear to you, I am poisoned. There is wickedness in that apple's flesh." He shook his head. "You are a good knight, Sir Crespin, but far too trusting. It is the beast's will to tempt us with false promises of unnatural strength. To eat of this fruit is folly. It will either damn us like Adam, or ensnare us here forever like the food of Faerie."

"I cannot say whether it is ill or no," said Sir Crespin, "but it is indeed a marvel. Say what you will, but I believe our host is an honest soul. We must show some gratitude."

Sir Alain held out his hand. "If Sir Bertran will not eat the apple, I beg you give it to me. I have need of it. I do not waste time fretting over demons and faeries."

"Very well," said Sir Crespin, giving him the apple. "But I am surprised you are hungry already, Alain?"

"It is not for hunger that I feast," said Sir Alain, tearing through the apple with great relish, "but for hardiness. The more we eat, the sooner we shall be a match for the dragon."

Nine more days passed. The dragon's hunger showed no signs of diminishing.

Each knight dutifully carried out his task to fetch the pail of blood. Each time, he was granted an abundance of apples and fresh water.

Sir Alain ate more apples than ever. Sir Bertran ate meager crusts of bread from their depleting rations. Sir

Crespin ate and drank no more or less than before, but always saved an apple for Sir Bertran. Without fail, Sir Bertran refused it.

Every night while the other men slept, Sir Alain quietly stole into the cold night air. He found whatever apples had gone uneaten and plucked them before they might vanish with the dawn. He ate three, six, nine, a dozen apples in a night. In the morning, the other knights thought Sir Alain seemed taller, stronger. His build was sturdier than a tree trunk, his muscles swollen like ripening fruit. His complexion grew more ruddy with each passing day. He hardly slept. While the dragon dozed, Sir Alain sat outside the cave and sharpened his sword against a stone. He did this until the blade was so keen, it could have sliced the very peak off *La Corne du Monde*.

A whole month went by. Upon an eve when it was Sir Alain's turn, the dragon lay sleeping in its chamber as usual. It awoke to the sound of, "Arise, dragon!" But when it sniffed the spot where its supper should have been, it smelled no blood. Instead, it detected the odor of sharp steel. Dragons have a keen sense of smell for all prized substances of the deep earth.

"*Where is my sssupper, sir knight?*" growled the dragon.

Sir Alain laughed. "You will sup no longer, dragon, nor see the light of moon and stars again! I have eaten richly of the fruit you so foolishly left us in great store. Now I am stronger than ten men, stronger even than you! I have come to win the freedom of my brothers and myself. I have come to rid this land of your foul presence."

With a single blow, Sir Alain sliced open the dragon's scaly breast. The dragon howled in pain. Sir Alain laughed again and prepared for the next stroke. But no sooner had he raised his sword than the dragon's breast healed over as quickly as hot wax cools in water. In a flash, the dragon swiped at Sir Alain's breast. The knight fell gasping and gurgling. Blood poured from his open wound. His body shuddered. Then he lay still, and was dead.

Sir Crespin and Sir Bertran returned from brushing the horses to find Sir Alain stretched out before the mouth of the cave. He was pale as alabaster and colder than steel. No stain of blood showed upon him. His wound was clean. His hands were bound by his black sash to the hilt of his sword. A sliver coin had been placed over each of his closed eyelids.

The knights wept and prayed for their fallen friend. The next morning, they buried him beneath a cairn of stones. They placed his sword point-down in the ground behind his head like a cross. Neither man spoke to the other. Each kept separate counsel in his own heart as to the cause of Sir Alain's fate.

The two remaining knights continued to take turns at the well, alternating every other day. Since the death of their comrade, Sir Bertran had grown more thin and starved than ever, refusing to eat at all. His face was white as a winding sheet. By night, he slept fitfully and murmured to himself; by day, he sat at the edge of the cliff in front of the cave, staring down the steep mountainside and clutching his shield to his body.

Sir Crespin ate and drank the same as always, one apple and one cup of water at a time. He continued to offer apples to Sir Bertran, and still Sir Bertran refused them.

An evening came when it was Sir Bertran's turn to go to the well. He filled the pail, brought it back to the cave, and left it in the dragon's chamber. But he did not call out to the dragon. Instead, he left the cave and began to walk the path down the mountain.

Sir Crespin saw this and called out in alarm. "Sir Bertran! Where are you going? Do not leave!"

Sir Bertran turned. His eyes were wide, and his skin

was stretched taut against his skull. "You would have me stay?" he croaked. "I will dwell no more with this monster! It has been the death of Sir Alain, and soon it shall be the death of you and me. Its hunger is never-ceasing!"

"But what will you do?" asked Sir Crespin. "Where will you go? Come, brother, sit with me and eat. You are sick and need rest."

"I do not have time to rest!" sputtered Sir Bertran. Flecks of spittle flew from his parched lips. "Every day we tarry here is another day we suffer this beast to live. One day, Crespin, one day when we join Sir Alain in heaven or in hell, there will be no one left to feed the dragon its ghastly milk. And then what? More slaughter! It will resume its evil ways and hunt the sons of man in the valley below. I tell you, I cannot remain here. I will flee the mountain. I will seek the aid of the king, and when an army is raised, we shall defeat the dragon together. One man may not have the power to slay it, but our might lies in numbers! Join me now, or stay if you wish, but do not try to stop me! I am going."

"Wait, brother Bertran!" cried Sir Crespin. But Sir Bertran was already out of sight, clambering down the mountain with his shield strapped to his arm.

Sir Crespin knelt down on the hard earth and said a

silent prayer for his comrade.

No sooner had Sir Bertran ran a little ways, than the clear streams along the path began to change. The waters ran thick and dark. They bubbled like tar and gave forth an evil vapor that burned his nostrils and blinded his eyes. The apple trees changed too. They turned black, sprouting thorns as long and sharp as lances. The branches dropped to the ground and writhed in circles. They trailed and twined around Sir Bertran's ankles, forming tangled thickets on every side. Sir Bertran frantically bashed his shield against them, but it was all in vain. The branches coiled around him tighter and tighter. Briars slashed him raw. At last, one huge spike, the length of a man's arm, punctured his shield and pierced him through the heart.

Thus was Sir Bertran forever entrapped in the embrace of a thousand thorns. The vines merged and melded into a single tree: his tomb. The tree bore hard red apples, and its fruit was bitter.

Alone now, Sir Crespin carried the silver pail to the well of blood every day.

The apple trees grew green and golden for him each evening. The dragon slept peacefully by day, and by night showed Sir Crespin no malice. At times, when the sun burned brightest in the sky and despair burned quietly in his heart, Sir Crespin perched atop a rock by the well and gazed down at the city below. Whether he would ever see another living man, he knew not. But so long as he remained steadfast in his duties to the dragon, the folk of Valbrume would be safe.

Many months passed. One evening, when the air was hot and the wind was still, Sir Crespin went up the hill to fill the pail with blood.

When he returned to the cave, he laid the pail upon the ground. As always, he called out, "Arise, dragon!"

But there came no reply.

He called out again. "Arise, dragon! It is sundown, and I am come with your supper."

But still the cave was silent. It was also, he now noticed, no longer hot and smoky. It felt cool and fresh and damp.

"You will find no dragon here," said a voice like sweet music echoing over white marble.

Light flooded the cave. Sir Crespin shielded his eyes. Squinting through his fingers, he beheld a lady clad in fine white samite, holding aloft a silver lantern.

Her skin was smooth and fair, flawless as a pearl. The only blemish upon her was a single jagged scar across her collarbone. Her hair was black as deepest night, and her eyes a warm bronze. "I have regained my true aspect," she said.

Sir Crespin knelt upon one knee. "Lady," he said in wonder, "who are you? Were you truly the dragon who dwelt in this cave?"

"I am Isobel, daughter of the lord of Valbrume," she said. "I was to be wed to the earl of another fiefdom, a sorcerer of sinister arts. When I rejected the betrothal, the earl flew into a rage. He placed upon my body a curse that I should be twisted into the shape of a loathsome dragon, ever hungering for human flesh. I was banished to the heights of *La Corne du Monde* and have remained here ever since." Her eyes dropped to the floor. Heavy sorrow filled her voice. "In my heart, I felt shame and revulsion each time I ate a man of Valbrume. Some of them were my friends and kinsmen. But the dragon nature compelled me to do things I could not control. I was trapped in a nightmare."

"But how is it you are now restored?" asked Sir Crespin.

"The earl placed upon the mountain many enchantments both cruel and kind, as you have seen. Many who climbed the mountain tried to slay me, or flee from me. Many more entered the same bargain I presented you with, and suffered the same fate as your two companions. The curse could only be lifted by a man so honest and loyal that he would feed me blood for a year and a day without fail." She looked up and gave a small smile. Her eyes were flooded with sadness and relief. "For what you have done, and what you have endured, I am forever thankful. Such hardship and solitude is not an easy thing to bear. I know this all too well."

The knight bowed his head low. "Lady, what I have endured this year and a day is a small thing compared with what you must have suffered these many years. I have horses still, and will accompany you back to Valbrume if you so desire."

"I thank you for your kindness, sir knight," said Isobel. "But for me, Valbrume is too full of memory and heartache now. I cannot go home. Rather would I sail to some fresh isle where the dragon of *La Corne du Monde* is unheard of."

"Then I shall go with you to ensure your safe passage," replied Sir Crespin.

Isobel smiled wider now and stretched out her hand. Sir Crespin took it and gently kissed her slim white fingers. He said, "I have traveled many roads, seeking solace in some final haven. But perhaps my feet were not meant to rest so soon. Perhaps they were meant to cross paths with another, and join in that journey. I ask you, humbly, would you have me by your side as you make your way through the world? Perhaps we may both find what we seek."

Isobel beamed. "Indeed, I would not refuse such a loyal companion as yourself."

She lead him out of the cave. Sir Crespin seated her on a horse. Just as he was about to mount his own steed, Isobel touched his shoulder.

"Wait," she said. "There is one horse that has no rider. Perhaps we should not leave his saddle so empty?" She grinned slyly.

"I do not understand," said Sir Crespin.

"Go to the inner chamber where I slept. In the cave wall you will find another, smaller chamber. Take my lantern with you."

Sir Crespin did as he was bid. Inside the cave, he found a low hollow set into the wall. Within it sat a wooden chest girt with silver. He carried the chest out and set it on the ground.

"Open it," said Isobel.

Sir Crespin unclasped the lid and opened it. He gasped. Inside the chest lay heaps of coins, piles of rubies, plus rings and cups and crowns aplenty to fill three caves; yet from the outside, the chest was small and as light as a box of feathers. It was easily borne upon the horse's back without strain.

"This was once my dowry," said Isobel, "but now I am free to give it away, however and to whomever I choose. Consider it a reward—no, a gift. A gift betokening gratitude... and friendship."

"Lady," said Sir Crespin, "I value honor beyond all the riches of this world. And no greater honor can I imagine than to have released such a kind-hearted soul from captivity. Let us instead share this bountiful wealth, and see where fortune may lead us."

And so Sir Crespin and the lady Isobel rode together down the Horn of the World in pursuit of the open sea. The people of Valbrume were troubled by dragons no more.

3

THE WIDOW BY THE SEA

The ocean is a fickle creature. Its touch is by turns savage and tender. It may yield abundance or bring desolation. It bestows a blessing or a curse as quickly as the turning of the tides—sometimes both upon the same person.

At the far end of the beach lies a ruined cottage. Perhaps you've seen it. All that remains now is a rectangular array of rubble. But it was once a proper cottage, long ago. An old widow lived there for many years.

Before you suppose too much, do not pity her. She was the sort who scorned pity. She worked hard all her days. And there was a time when, long after the tempests made a widow of her, she did not live alone.

Every day, the widow slung a basket over her back and scoured the sands for brine-drenched seaweed. Once a week, she hobbled the mile from shore to village to sell her wares. Farmers spread the seaweed on poor soil to make their fields fertile. They paid the widow a fair price for it; at least, it was enough for her to get by on with a little thrift. When her week's harvest was sold, she would totter up to the tiny cliff-top church to pray. She always made sure to light a candle at the Virgin Mary's shell-shaped grotto before hobbling home again.

Sometimes she found more than just seaweed. Now and again the tides retched forth shipwreck debris. A day's takings might include a spyglass, an astrolabe, a chest, a chair, tables, trinkets, textiles, or at the very least, an empty sugar sack. The widow dutifully gathered up these relics of the nameless drowned. She took the smaller, lighter items back to the village to fetch a few coins. The heavier pieces she dragged across the sand to her cottage and kept for her own. Thus her humble croft was furnished as richly as a captain's cabin. The heavy odor of fish and salt clung to every object in the dim smoky room.

One bright summer's day, the widow was out gathering seaweed when she spied something odd peeking out of the sand nearby. It looked hard and smooth, its reddish brown surface reflecting the midday sun. Kneeling down stiffly, the widow dug the object up and held it close to her face. "A lovely little box!" she exclaimed. For indeed, it was a small polished rosewood chest set with brass clasps. She pried it open. Inside were a slender sable brush, a few tubes of paint, and a small china dish.

"Watertight. Dry as a bone," she remarked. She rifled through the contents. "Still some paint left. And the wood is so handsome. Only a little scuffed. I'm sure I could get a pretty penny for it." So she put the box in her basket and set off for home.

Back at the cottage, she buffed the paintbox with an oilcloth until it gleamed good as new. She admired the rosewood's warm color. "Perhaps I'll not sell it after all," she thought. "Not yet. It's a fine piece, and I like it. I'll keep it on the table for now."

That Saturday she sold her seaweed, prayed at the chapel, and lit a candle to the blue-veiled Virgin. Then she returned to the shore. But instead of going straight home, she sat down on the sand to rest a while. Her back ached. Her feet hurt. And though she would confess it to no one, her heart was sore.

She idly pushed handfuls of sand into little mounds and valleys. After a time, the shapes merged to resemble the crude figure of a man lying on the beach. "How I wish there was someone to help me gather seaweed," she mused, placing a clump of wrack on the sand-man's head for hair. "And how I wish I could cook that someone a nice meal every day to thank them for their hard work," she said, placing periwinkles on the sand-man's face for eyes. "And how I wish," she whispered, "to have someone to talk to in the day, and..." She pressed in a pair of scallops for ears and a pink crab claw for lips. "It's a sorry thing," she said to the finished face, "to come home to an empty cottage every night."

She wept a little. Seven tears fell from her cheek upon the sand-man's breast. The widow dabbed her eyes with a handkerchief and rose to her feet. She walked home, ate her supper, and went to bed.

The next morning, she went out to gather more seaweed.

The tide had erased all traces of the sand figure. The widow sighed and set about her work.

She had not been laboring long when a high cry pierced the wind. The widow looked up. She saw nothing. "Must be a curlew's call," she thought, and carried on with her task.

After a few minutes, the cry came again. It was harsh and barking. The widow looked up. Nothing again. "Must be a seal upon the rocks," she muttered, and went back to work.

A moment later, the cry sounded a third time. It was a long groan, low and anguished. The widow looked up. This time there was no mistaking the source of the sound: lying before her in the sand was a young man, naked and shivering. His grey eyes rolled back in his head, flashing feverishly. His long green-black hair was soaked with seawater. The sun burned his bare white skin.

"Poor soul!" cried the widow. She dropped her basket and threw her shawl over his shaking body. He sat up and let her wrap the shawl tightly about him.

Holding fast to his arm, the widow carefully helped the stranger stand and walked him back to her cottage.

She laid him in her bed and drew up the covers. "Sleep now," she said. "The sea has spared you. Death will not take you, so long as I can help it."

The stranger slept deeply through the night. He slept all the next morning too. When the widow left to gather seaweed in the afternoon, she did not stay out for long. "I mustn't leave him out of my sight. He needs a good deal of tending to." She hurried home to find him still fast asleep.

"I'll cook some supper," she thought. "The smell should wake his appetite." She busied herself over the hearth, boiling and seasoning a pot of potatoes. She sat down and ate her portion. The stranger slept on.

"I'll build up the fire," she thought. "Maybe the warmth will put some life back in his limbs." So she put a hunk of driftwood on the hearth. The fire blazed merrily and warmed the cottage up in a trice. But the stranger slept on.

"It's no use," she sighed. "I'll have to sit up and watch over him till he wakens. I'm not sleeping on the floor again like last night." So the widow sat at the table and bided her time. She darned a few holey socks. When that was done, she patched a tear in her shawl. When that was done, she said, "The moon hasn't traveled far across the sky! There's hours left until dawn. What's to be done in the meantime?"

Then she remembered the paintbox on the table.

She opened up the little rosewood chest and took out the tubes of paint, the sable paintbrush, and the china dish. With a little struggle, she twisted the tubes open and squeezed a dot of each color onto the dish: red, blue, yellow, black, and white. She moistened the paintbrush in a kettle and stirred the dots of paint around the dish. New colors emerged: swirls of green, orange, purple, grey, and brown. "Lovely!" she thought. "But I can't just let this paint dry on good china. What else is there to brush it on?"

She searched the cottage and found a flat piece of driftwood beside the hearth. She washed the brush clean and dabbed a bit of fresh white paint onto the smooth, wind-worn wood. A little thumbnail moon took shape, just like the one outside her window. "Not bad," she admired. "Could use some stars." She dipped her brush again and painted seven twinkling stars around the crescent moon. "That's better," she said. "Hm, what next?"

She looked over at the man sleeping soundly in her bed beneath the window. "Poor thing," she sighed. She dipped her brush again. Now she painted a face with its eyes closed peacefully under a starry moonlit night. "There," she said, filling in the last dab of hair. "Doesn't do him justice. But it's a fair start all the same."

Just then, the man stirred beneath the blanket. He

stretched his arms and legs and let out a soft sigh. He opened his eyes.

"Bless me, you're awake at last!" cried the widow. She quickly hid the driftwood painting in a covered pot on the mantle. "I thought you'd go on sleeping for a hundred years!"

The man sat up unsteadily. He tried to stand. The blanket fell away.

"Goodness!" exclaimed the widow. "I almost forgot—you're still naked as a newborn! Here, let's fix that."

She dragged a heavy wooden trunk out from under the bed. Rummaging through it, she extracted a thick woolen sweater and a pair of old trousers. "My husband was a bit more broad in the shoulders than you, but it'll have to do," she said.

The man said nothing. He clumsily pulled the clothing on as though dressing was a custom with which he was long out of practice.

"It'll soon be morning," she said. "I expect you'll be wanting breakfast. You missed out on potatoes, but I can stir up a bowl of porridge." She set some oats and milk on to boil. "You needn't stand there gawping, lad, sit down!"

The man did as he was told and seated himself at the table.

"You're a quiet one, make no mistake," said the widow. "What port do you hail from? Did your ship go down in that terrible squall last week? It's a miracle you're still alive."

The man made no reply. He watched with interest as she made the porridge.

"Never mind," said the widow. "I'll say no more about it. Lord knows you sailors have been to hell and back on those waves... and you're one of the lucky ones. Anyway, all that matters now is there's air in your lungs and land under your feet." She nodded with surety.

The man devoured the porridge set before him. When he'd scraped the last morsels from the bowl, he stared up at the widow with the pleading intensity of a hungry dog.

"All right, all right! If it's an appetite you have, I'll not let you starve!" said the widow. She fixed another bowl of porridge.

The man wolfed it down as ravenously as he had the first. He looked up again, his mute request unmistakable.

"You'll eat me out of house and home!" she cried, putting another pot of porridge on to boil. After the third bowl, the stranger seemed satisfied. He leaned back in his chair. His gaze turned to the sun peeping in through the window above the bed.

"Ah, you'll be needing some fresh air, no doubt?"

asked the widow. "A bit of moving about will do you good."

The stranger stood up and walked to the door.

"Now see here! Wait a minute!" said the widow. "I can't just let you leave like that. You're in no fit state to set off into the world on your own yet. Besides," she added, "I need to go to the village to buy something for supper. I'm sure you won't say no to another meal!"

She leaned against the table edge, frowning in thought. "I tell you what: why don't you take my basket out and start picking up the sea wrack that's washed ashore." She grinned and wagged a finger at him. "Oh, I can tell you're no stranger to an honest day's work. If you're going to recover your strength by emptying my larder, you might as well earn your keep! It's about time I had some help around here."

She clucked her tongue as she pulled on her shawl and tucked a small coin purse in the pocket of her apron. "Now, don't stray far. Stay where you can keep the cottage in sight. Oh, and if you find anything else of value, throw it in the basket—so long as it's not another half-drowned sailor!"

When the widow reached the village, the first stop she made was to see the miller.

"That's enough flour to fill a mountain, missus!" exclaimed the miller as he weighed out the widow's order.

"So?" countered the widow. She glared at him sourly. Then she paid for her flour and left.

Next she went to the fishmonger.

"If all my customers had your appetite, missus, there'd be nothing left in the sea!" warned the fishmonger.

"The sea's big enough to feed us all," said the widow with a sniff. She paid for her fish and left.

Then she visited the greengrocer's.

"Eating for two, missus?" sneered the greengrocer's wife.

"Whist! I can eat what I like, and *you* can eat my money if you don't want it in your pocket!" said the widow. She paid for her vegetables and left.

Lastly, she went to the cobbler's shop to buy a pair of large, sturdy boots.

The cobbler raised an eyebrow. "Surely, missus, your cottage hasn't grown too small?" he chuckled. "Will you be moving into one of these shoes, like the old wifey in the rhyme?"

"You'll take a crown for these boots, or I'll give you a boot to the crown!" snapped the widow. She paid for the shoes and tottered back to the shore. She stopped now and again to lay down her day's purchases and rest.

When she arrived home, she discovered her strange guest had filled not one, not two, but three baskets full of seaweed. He was still combing the shore for other gleanings. "Dear me!" cried the widow. "When I told you to do a bit of work, I didn't mean for you to be at it all day! Here, set that basket down and help me with these packages."

The man did as he was told. He picked up the widow's entire stack of goods with one arm as though they weighed nothing.

"Oh. Er, thank you," said the widow. "I see your strength is coming back already! We'll bring these baskets in too and see if you found anything interesting."

The man picked up the three full baskets in his other arm and stepped inside.

The widow made a fire in the hearth and lit an oil lamp on the table. "Now, let's have a look," she said, digging through one of the baskets. She pulled out a few heaps of seaweed before coming upon some broken wooden planks and a few shreds of canvas sail. "My, my, looks like the remains of some unfortunate ship? Was it yours, perhaps? No, never mind. Let's not talk about that. At any rate, I'm sure we'll find some good use for these scraps. *Waste not what can be used anew*, I always say. But we need to let them dry first. Here," she said, handing him a soggy bundle, "prop the wood outside the cottage, and hang the sails on the clothesline. If we have another clear day tomorrow, they'll soon be dry."

Next she sorted through her stack of purchases. "When you've finished, sit down and see if these shoes fit. I'll get started on supper. Let's see, let's see, what to make first? A bit of this? A bit of that? Or a little bit of everything?" She bustled about the hearth, giddy with indecision. "We could have quite a feast, couldn't we?"

The next day was bright and hot. The widow made her guest a huge pot of porridge for breakfast and went outside to check on the wood and canvas. "Goodness me, they're bone dry already!" she exclaimed. She looked about the beach. No more seaweed had washed ashore in the night. There was no work for her to do at home, save cook all day. "Yesterday's catch may as well go to market," she muttered to herself. "But what shall I give *him* to do while I'm gone? They say idle hands do the Devil's work."

She thought a bit. Then she had an idea. "I'm going into town again!" she called through the open cottage window. "There's a box of nails on the shelf, and a hammer on the wall. See what you can patch up. The chairs creak, and the bed squeaks, and the roof beams are sagging. That'll keep you busy!"

In the village, the farmers were surprised to see the widow bringing so much seaweed so early in the week. "To be sure, she has a faery helper!" they joked to one another.

"Do you want to buy it or not?" said the widow.

The farmers exchanged bemused glances and said no more about it. They bought the seaweed until her baskets were empty and her coin purse full.

Next, she visited the tailor's shop. She picked out a charming sky-blue dress of fine linen.

"Begging your pardon, missus," said the tailor, "but could I interest you in something a bit more... practical? That frock is far too delicate to be dredging the shores in. But then I suppose you'll be wanting it to wear to church? Still, if I may say so, it's cut in a fashion meant for ladies a bit, well... *younger*."

"If you think you can tell me how to dress myself, I'll have you dressed for the roasting spit! Insolent boy." She paid for the dress, and changed into it behind a screen.

Lastly, she went to the weaver's cottage. She bought a soft new woolen shawl the color of the midnight sea. She threw some coins at the weaver before he had a chance to make a comment. With the shawl draped elegantly about her shoulders, she swept out of the weaver's cottage and trod lightly down the lane. Her journey homewards passed shorter than ever. She was so eager, she forgot to stop at the chapel to light a candle to the Virgin.

When she arrived home, she was astonished to see how well the cottage looked. The stranger's handiwork made the squeaking chairs silent, the creaking bed quiet, and the sagging beams straight. The whole cottage stood tall and proud. And the man was still working.

"What a talent you have!" she exclaimed over the rhythmic hammer-fall. "Are you sure you're a sailor and not a master carpenter? What're you working on now? Surely there can't be *that* much in this old place to fix up?"

The man put a few finishing taps to his project and looked up at her at last. Without a word, he handed her a stack of square wooden frames. Each frame had a piece of canvas stretched over it and was nailed fast at the edges.

"What's this?" the widow asked. She turned the objects over in her hands and looked to him for some explanation. "Are these made from those bits of wood and sails?"

The man nodded.

"But what are they for?" she asked.

The man reached over and opened the paintbox on the table. He took out the brush and held it up.

"Oh!" she cried. "You clever thing!" She flashed him a beaming smile. Suddenly, her face reddened. She glanced up at the mantle. The covered pot appeared to be untouched. Perhaps he hadn't found the little driftwood painting after all. She shook her head and made an effort to smile again. "Oh, this is grand, just grand! Thank you, really. What a clever thing to do." She reached over to squeeze his hand.

Yet all she felt in her grasp was a fistful of sand. Quickly, she dropped his hand and stared at her own. Her palm and fingers were covered in a fine layer of white grit. She looked up at him. "Dear me," she said absently, "you must be quite a mess from all that work." She wiped her hand on her apron and shivered abruptly, as though jolting from a half-dream. "Go on outside and wash up. I'll fix us some supper. Afterwards we can try out one of these lovely presents you've made me."

After supper, the setting sun bathed the horizon in a warm rosy hue. The widow had her guest drag a chair in front of the cottage so she could sit and paint outdoors.

First, she covered the canvas' lower half in a dark marine color—somewhere between the blue of her new shawl and the green-black of her companion's hair. Then she painted the top half a gold-suffused pink, punctuated by a red semicircle in the center for the sun. She blotted a bit of orange over the water's surface, and finished with a few swipes of wispy grey clouds. "There," she said, eyeing her project. "What do you think?"

The man seemed not to hear her. He was idly pacing the tide line, leaving spirals in the sand with his footsteps.

She wanted to paint his silhouette into the picture. She watched his dark backlit form bend with the breeze and breathe with the tide. She was about to set brush to canvas again when the man suddenly looked at her.

She put the brush down at once.

He walked over and studied the painting in her lap. Then he looked up at the horizon. Then back down at the picture. Then he looked at her. He smiled.

She thought her heart would crack in two with joy.

Each day, she painted another picture: images of the ever-changing horizon, of the dunes and their feathered grasses, of the rocks in their sharp starkness. Each painting delighted the man even more. His face, which in daytime was impassive as stone, lit up at night like the evening star to see his hostess' newest creations.

The widow gave him no end of work to do. Sometimes it was to help her gather seaweed. More often, it was to fix something around the cottage that she insisted was broken or worn out. The roof was re-thatched, the floors scrubbed clean of grime, and a low stone enclosure built around the house. The man showed no signs of tiring.

Evenings they spent eating fresh suppers of the finest foods the widow could buy (he sometimes eating two or three); then they would retire to the front of the cottage, the scent of salt and baked sand drifting on the balmy breeze. The widow painted, and the man dreamily wandered the beach until the sun was set.

One night, the widow sat up late by the fire while the man lay sleeping in a cot beside her bed. She watched him, his breathing slow and sure and peaceful. She smiled to herself contentedly.

Certain he was deeply asleep, she crept over to the mantle and removed the hidden piece of driftwood from the covered pot. "I've had a bit of practice," she thought. "I'm sure I could make a few improvements to this one."

The canvases were wonderful to work upon, but the little sable brush never glided so smoothly as it did upon bare driftwood. She adorned the edges of the painting with details of shells and vegetation. She added a body to the head and, on impulse, placed above the figure's shoulders a suggestion of fiery wings in the colors of sunset.

It was much easier to study her model when he was asleep. She sat closer and examined his face in careful detail. It was uncanny how pale he was. His features were as finely curved as a seashell's. They had a light of their own, like chalk cliffs reflecting the noonday sun. He was, in a way, too perfect. And now, those features seemed sharper, clearer, more beautiful than the day she'd found him. Had her eyesight reversed its inevitable dimming? She knelt down and brushed a lock of hair from his face. With utmost delicacy, she laid her fingertips on his cheekbone.

Her hand sank into his face with no resistance. She drew back in horror. Her fingers were covered in sand. The man's face was unblemished and serene as always.

"I'm going mad," she whispered. Her jaw quivered. She clutched her chest and breathed heavily. "I'm losing my senses... just as they always said I would." She wrung her hands in her apron and paced the room. She shook herself again. "No. No, it's all right. It's nothing. I'll wash up and go to bed. All will be right in the morning."

When the canvases finally ran out one day, the widow declared, "I must have something else to paint upon. You know, these old cottage walls are looking bare. Wouldn't it be nice if we dressed them up a bit?"

The two companions dragged furniture outside, scrubbed the walls, and swept the floors. For weeks, by sunlight and moonlight and lamplight and candlelight, the widow painted the walls with murals of ships and shores, islands and cliffs, seas full of stars. She painted every creature of land and water she could think of. She painted beings that existed only in the tales of her girlhood: water-horses, sea-serpents, selkies with human faces and seal's eyes. She painted the villagers going about their daily lives. She painted the chapel, the windswept trees, and the churchyard. Over all this, she painted the image of the Blessed Virgin; no longer confined to a humble grotto, Mary's blue veil stretched from wall to wall in rolling waves that embraced the whole of Creation.

The man's face could not contain his delight as the dull cottage walls came to vibrant life.

As for herself, the widow had never before known such bliss. As long as she had things to paint, and her friend to paint for, she would surround herself with beauty. She would be happy, and she would not feel old.

Summer waned. The days grew shorter. A chill, biting wind blew in from across the sea.

"Go and see if you can find some driftwood," said the

widow one morning. "We need plenty to burn unless we want to wake up tomorrow covered in frost! I'm going to the village to buy food. Maybe a bottle of whisky too." She chuckled. "That'll warm us up for sure!" She set off for town, leaving the man to his task.

She returned with her arms full of goods. When she entered the cottage, she found the man standing with his back to the door. A pile of driftwood lay at his feet, and another pile burned away in the hearth. In his hands, the man held the little piece of wood that bore his portrait.

The packages fell from the widow's arms. "How did you find that?" she gasped. The bottle of whisky slipped from her grasp and crashed to the floor. Broken glass and spirits pooled about her feet. "I told you to find wood for the fire," she said. "I didn't mean..." Her hand flew to her face. "You did exactly as I asked you to," she whispered. "Just as you always do..." She reached for the piece of driftwood, but the man held it close. He would not look away from it. His brow furrowed.

"Oh, say something, won't you?" she pleaded. "I'm sorry! I'm so very sorry. Please, speak to me! For God's sake, why won't you speak?"

At last, he looked up. His eyes held no anger or embarrassment. Their focus was soft and distant.

Without aggression, he cast the painting into the fire.

He sidestepped the widow and walked straight out the door.

"Wait!" cried the widow. "Where are you going?" She stumbled after him across the beach, tripping through rocks and sand.

He walked so swiftly that he seemed to glide across the shore. He waded into the water up to his waist and stretched out his arms. His fingers brushed the white foam on the waves. He tilted his head up to the sky.

The widow reached the tide line and fell to her knees. "Wait!" she cried. "Come back!"

He turned his face to her. He shook his head. Then he smiled—a pale, sad smile.

Just then, a great wave, green and glimmering, rose up from the sea. It barreled towards him.

"Come back!" the widow screamed. "Come back! You'll drown!"

The wave arced to a staggering height. Then, with a deafening crash, it fell and struck the man full across the body. Water flowed right through him. His head, his torso, his limbs—all of him dissolved. In the span of a single breath, he was gone.

The widow cried out. Seven drops of seawater fell upon her face like tears. She heaved herself up and waded into the water. Thrashing and beating at the sea, she screamed, "Why? Why? You have stolen *everything* from me! What more must I give up before you grant me some peace?" The roaring, spray-filled winds gave no answer. They swept around her from all directions, suffocating her cries.

Another wave rose up. It hovered for an instant. Then it fell down upon her. But the impact was gentle. It did not even throw her off balance. The water felt clear and ice-cold. It filled her mouth and lungs. Soon it filled her whole body. When the wave receded, she turned and walked down the shore—away from the cottage, never stopping to look back.

That was a long time ago. Fishermen tell stories of ghosts, merfolk, and creatures of the deep to put a touch of fear and delight in the hearts of land-dwellers. Of course, few believe those legends now. We know so much more about the sea than our ancestors did. Its mysteries are not so mysterious anymore.

And yet, on that long white shore where the moon writes its name on the sands, some folk swear they have seen a strange shade out among the rocks. Bent and frail, wrapped in a shawl the color of the hungry ocean, it wanders aimlessly. It can only be seen from a distance. Some call it a ghost; others say it is the "physical manifestation of some great despair"—the feelings of a bereft woman made real. She is forever gazing out at the horizon, waiting for a ship that will never come in.

But that is not entirely true. They forget that everyone the ocean claims a piece of must one day return to it. The woman wandering the shores does not grieve. She does not feel anything. That is because it is only her shadow that walks among the rocks—an echo of the past, nothing more. Her soul, on the other hand, has left this land long ago. It is a wave on the sea, free and fluid. It floats among countless thousands of other waves. They are ageless, sorrowless. Nothing can contain them, and they are never lonely.

4

THE GOLDEN ARROW

Noble Ademar rode across the plain as swift as a streaking comet. With hair like waves of beaten bronze, he was more handsome than a summer's day. His smile was easy, and his gaze hard. He sat tall and proud in the saddle of a white steed, thundering through leagues of lush grass to arrive at the doors of the Hall of the Mighty.

Horns trumpeted full and clear as Ademar ascended

the steps. Pages ran hurriedly to match his long-legged gait. Red and silver hunting hounds bounded alongside him, barking to herald their master's return. The doors of the Hall swung forth. Maidens of surpassing beauty, richly garbed in bejeweled gowns, crowded breathlessly among the four corners of the hall. Ademar climbed the velvet-draped dais to take his seat in a massive oaken throne. Cup-bearers filled his goblet to the brim with intoxicating green mead. Behind him, pine logs crackled in a cavernous hearth.

Surveying the feast that awaited him, Ademar smiled inwardly. With great majesty, he arose to his feet. The assembled company of knights and ladies bowed as one. Ademar lifted his cup on high. The fire in the hearth cast a halo of gold round his head. He shone like the sun itself.

"Glory unto the Mighty!" he cried.

"Then, now, and evermore!" came the chorused reply.

Six princes there were in Arbethia. Each governed his own small dominion. Each kept a standing army, yet all swore oaths of fealty to Damon, King of Arbethia. In times of need, the six princes summoned their armies without hesitation and fought alongside their beloved sovereign. There was no greater duty, nor higher honor, than to fight—and if need be, die—for Arbethia's king.

Damon had no sons; thus, the line of succession fell to the princes. The boldest of the six was Prince Ademar. He was last in line to the throne but closest in the king's confidence. Ademar was his majesty's favorite. A trusted friend, he was as near to a son as could be.

It came to pass upon a year when grain covered the Black Steppes in carpets of gold, that a warlord from the south rose up to wage battle on Arbethia. It is said his armies were a terror to behold. It is also said he was born with the strength of an ox and the eyes of a hawk: he could slay his target from a league away with a single arrow.

The princes of Arbethia assembled their armies upon the Black Steppes. King Damon led the charge. The battle lasted a fortnight. Rivers of blood coursed from both sides, feeding the wheat fields until golden grain turned to rust.

At last, Arbethia gained the upper hand. The army from the south was crippling fast. Prince Ademar rode beside King Damon, scanning the horizon to plan a final attack. Suddenly, the prince spied a figure in the distance. It was the warlord, his wild hair a storm of grey beneath an iron helm. In his left hand the warlord held a bow. His right arm was drawn back, preparing to launch a bright golden arrow.

"Sire, look out!" cried Prince Ademar. He jumped from his horse and pulled the king down with him.

Like a bolt of fire, the arrow flew straight at King Damon. Inches from his breast, it turned sharply to one side and shot back from whence it came. Neither man saw where it landed.

"Faithful Ademar!" cried the king. "I owe you my life." He embraced the prince.

There was a great commotion at the other end of the battlefield. The enemy slowed its advance to a dead halt. Dozens of warriors gathered in a huddle, and the air fell silent.

"Sire, stay here," said Prince Ademar. "I must find out what has happened."

Ademar rode to the huddle and dismounted. Drawing his sword, he parted his way to the center of the crowd. There upon the ground lay the warlord, crumpled in a heap. He was dead. Blood matted his heavy black cloak. His iron breastplate was shattered. Ademar stepped close to the body, gazing on it in amazement. The arrow of gold, the very arrow that had so nearly slain King Damon, was plunged deep into the warlord's left breast. Where the man's heart should have been was nothing but a black, smoking hole. Flakes of ash spiraled from it into the wind.

A victory feast was held at the royal palace. The six princes of Arbethia sat three on either side of King Damon and his wife, the fair Queen Apraksha. The Hall of the Mighty was full of wounded warriors. It was a bittersweet affair. Tears flowed for the dead, and mead flowed in happy remembrance of them.

Prince Ademar sat nearest the king. "I raise my glass to your good fortune, my lord," he said. "Your men did not fall in vain. With the southern warlord dead, and his descendents among our prisoners, the enemy's land belongs to you now. Surely you must reap some gladness from that?"

King Damon shook his head sadly. "Good Prince Ademar, now is not the time to admire the spoils of war. Tonight, my duty lies with those who have served me. To the men who sit before us, I bestow rewards of gold, furs, salt, wine, everlasting praise, and the renewed promise of protection. As for those who cannot join our earthly feast, I offer my blessing for a safe passage through the seas of heaven to the Valley of Victorious Dead. Truly, it is in their name that we hold this banquet."

When night waned into pale dawn, Ademar retired to his

guest quarters at the palace. He sat down upon the bed beside a bundle of furs. Unwrapping the bundle, he carefully withdrew the object it protected: an arrow, bone-slender, bright as mid-day, quivering as though alive. He'd plucked the arrow from the warlord's smoldering breast and claimed it for his own. Now that it was safe in his possession, he wished to know its true value.

Ademar wended his way down snaking palace corridors until he came to the chamber of the king's sorcerer. He knocked on the door.

A voice as dry as parchment croaked from within the chamber. "Give an old man some peace! It's nigh on morning, and I've only just gone to bed!"

"Wise old fellow, be not so hasty! It is I, Prince Ademar. I come seeking your esteemed counsel... and to share in the *bounties* of a battle well won." Ademar made sure to clink the bottle of wine in his hand against a coin pouch on his belt.

The door opened abruptly. "Generous Ademar!" exclaimed the sorcerer. The old white-beard flashed a sleepy smile at the prince. "Come in, come in. Your company is always welcome! Do sit down."

Ademar poured the sorcerer a plentiful cup. "I regret disturbing your rest at this hour, old friend," he said, "but I fear I have a burning curiosity that must be quenched. I recall how well-learned you are in the history of powerful objects. I hope I can depend upon you to help me untangle a little mystery. What do you know of enchanted weapons?"

"Weapons?" said the sorcerer, taking a long draught. "I know a thing or two about weapons. What sort of weapons are we talking about? Singing swords? Glass shields? Hammers hewn from giants' bones?"

"An arrow," said Prince Ademar. He poured the sorcerer another cupful. "In particular, *this* arrow." He parted the fur wrappings to reveal the treasure within.

The sorcerer shielded his face against the arrow's bright glare. Upon second glance, his eyes widened. He nearly dropped his wine. "Where did you find that?" he gasped.

"It came into my rightful keeping," said Ademar. "Its former owner is dead, but not by my hand. I assure you that the rest of the story is immaterial." He untied the heavy coin pouch from his belt and dropped it in the old man's lap. "I only wish to know where it was made; that, and whether it's worth more on my armory wall or speeding from my bow upon the battlefield."

"Well..." continued the sorcerer, weighing the bag of coins in his hands, "it is—it *was* known simply as the 'Golden Arrow.' It was forged by smiths of the east, men of a holy order. They took vows of silence and forsook the company of women. Their crafts were the finest in all the world. Each stroke from their hammers imbued metal with a high magic. It is said their keenest pursuit was to create a weapon that granted its owner everlasting life."

"And they achieved this in the making of the Golden Arrow?" asked Ademar.

"Not quite," said the sorcerer. "The arrow lends a kind of... limited immortality... at a price." He cleared his throat. "'*He shall never age, who possesses the arrow; neither can he die by poison, nor perish by a blade. Whomsoever he shoots at with single-minded purpose, he shall not miss, and shall inherit the victim's domain. The arrow can neither be sundered nor tarnished. Once it has stricken its target, it shall fly swiftly back to its master's quiver.*' But," the sorcerer added, nervously twisting his snowy beard, "'*he must not use it more than nine times in all; for upon the tenth time, the arrow will resolve against all odds to return and strike its master. The wound shall burn his heart unto ashes, and he shall die.*'"

Ademar was very quiet. He ran a finger gently down the length of the arrow. Its soft glow cast deep shadows under his cheekbones. "You say the owner cannot be poisoned?" he remarked at last.

"That's right," said the sorcerer. "Why?"

Ademar threw the furs back over the arrow and tucked the bundle under his arm. He grabbed the coin purse from the sorcerer's lap and got up to cross the chamber. At the door, he stopped and turned to look back. "It is unlucky for you, then, that you do not own it." With that, he turned on his heel and departed.

All of a sudden the old sorcerer's neck and limbs seized uncontrollably. His eyes bulged. His brow beaded with sweat, and his cheeks flushed ruby. Then, all color drained from his skin. He slumped sideways in his chair. His head rolled to one shoulder, and his countenance gaped blankly at the dying embers in the hearth. Blue-lipped, glassy-eyed, he was dead.

The perimeter of Arbethia is ten days' ride in a sunwise circuit. If the rider rests little, and the horse is of uncommon endurance, a week will suffice.

One morning, not long after the king's victory feast, the prince of Arbethia's northern fiefdom was slain while pursuing a wild boar. None of the hunting party confessed to firing the fatal shot. Such accidents were not unheard of. A man may easily mistake his fellow hunter for a beast where the trees grow thickest together.

The next day, the prince of the east was found dead upon his castle ramparts. He had suffered a deep wound to the head. There was no sign of the weapon, nor of the culprit.

The day after that, the prince who dwelt among the mountains was out training falcons. Without warning, he plunged off a precipice to his death. His servants grieved bitterly and cursed themselves for not being more vigilant of their master's safety. Their eyes had been on the hunting birds instead of on the prince. Still, the tragic accident came as a shock. He had always been as sure-footed as any mountain goat.

The next morning, the prince of the southern Steppes was found dead in his counting house. He was alone, save for the heaps of grain and gold coins upon which he bled in rivulets of red. The counting house had but one door. This was kept locked to the outside at all times. It also had a single window, only a hand's breadth wide and set high into the wall. For lack of any sounder justice, the last servant seen to have entered the counting house the night before was seized and put to death.

The following day, the prince of the westerly seaside realm tumbled over the railing of his own flagship. A flash of something like lightning had startled him. This baffled his crew, who had ever admired their prince for his stoutness of heart. Nonetheless, the waves that day were fierce indeed, and the crew was unable to retrieve the body from its watery grave. Some said they saw another flash of light skim the surface of the water just after the prince fell. This, they agreed, was surely his soul flying up to heaven.

A day later, the royal palace awoke in the middle of the night to the screams of Queen Apraksha. Every servant, from the lowest maid to the king's young new sorcerer, rushed into the royal bedchamber with candles and torches alight. The Queen, tangled in her bed-sheets, was red-faced with hysterics. King Damon lay peacefully upon the mattress. A wet scarlet stain bloomed from his right breast through the white linen of his shift.

At dawn, Arbethia woke to the burial of one king, and the crowning of another. A heavy air of mourning pervaded the land. But this mourning was mingled with a strange numbness and quiet surety that the mysterious deaths were finally at an end. "The new king will protect us with a steady hand," the people murmured to one another—though in truth, they knew not why. "He is right to rule alone. It was foolish to entrust power to so many weak princes who could not save themselves or King Damon. It is better this way."

King Ademar wed the Queen Apraksha when she was still clothed in her widow's raiments. She hardly spoke a word at the wedding feast. But even she could not avoid joining the throng of voices that responded to Ademar's boisterous toast:

"Glory unto the Mighty!"

"Then, now, and evermore!"

One of Ademar's first acts upon ascending the throne was to ensure his own continued safety. He did not fear betrayal by his people; possession of the arrow was safeguard against that. What he feared more than anything was his own instrument of power. He had already taken six lives with the Golden Arrow. Three more targets were permitted him before the arrow would exact its terrible price. Ademar was king of Arbethia now, but that did not mean he would never need to use the arrow again.

Ademar summoned the new sorcerer to the throne room. The young man bowed self-consciously before his king. "How may I serve you, my lord?"

"Tell me, mage," said Ademar, reclining upon his carven throne. He eyed a hanging tapestry with vague interest. "The kings of Arbethia are buried in the royal tombs beneath the palace, are they not?"

"They are, my lord," said the sorcerer, puzzled. The location of the tombs was common knowledge.

"And is it true you were present at our beloved King Damon's burial?"

"Yes, my lord..." the sorcerer replied. "Forgive me, sire, but you yourself were there. Why do you ask?"

Ademar continued casually. "And is it true that you were also present at King Damon's *other* burial?"

"*Other* b-burial, sire?" stammered the sorcerer.

"The one in which Damon's heart was laid to rest in the Grove of Kings," said Ademar.

"S-sire, how do you know of the Grove of Kings?"

"King Damon confided many things in me. We were very close, you know, like father and son. For instance, I know that in the great northern Wildwood, there is a stand of sacred birch trees that King Damon frequented. Often he would walk there, alone, to meditate and seek counsel with his ancestors. I also know that his father, and his father's father, and every king of Arbethia before them had his heart cut from his breast upon the hour of his death. Those hearts are stored up in vessels, and each vessel is lodged within the trunk of a birch tree."

The sorcerer gave no reply to confirm or deny this statement. His cheeks burned red, and he shifted uncomfortably on his feet.

"The heart is the seat of the soul," continued Ademar with a far-away look, "so long as the flesh of the heart remains intact. That is a skill only the king's sorcerer can wield: the art of preserving the heart from rotting away. Is that not correct?"

"It… it is," agreed the sorcerer.

"Then tell me, young mage, is it possible to store a man's heart away *before* his death?"

"*Before* death, sire?"

"Yes. Have you ever done this?"

"No sire, of course not. Do you… do you mean that you wish to—?"

"I wish for you to cut out my heart. Cut it from me as I am now, a living man. I want you to seal it away in a tree within the Grove of Kings."

"But sire, surely, that would kill you! What you ask is beyond dangerous. Even if the heart is preserved, no amount of magic could spare your body from death!"

"Then it seems I know more of magic than you do, boy," said Ademar with a coy smile. "Oh, don't look so surprised. People often assume that a skilled warrior's only accomplishments are on the battlefield. I'll have you know that as a child, I learned a great deal at the knee of your predecessor." He rang a bell to summon his pageboy. "Tell the Queen I'm afraid she must dine alone tonight," he said to the pageboy. "My sorcerer and I are taking an excursion to the woods to get better acquainted."

Under a delicate lacework of shade, Ademar strolled to

and fro among the Grove of Kings. He hummed a pleasant tune and smiled, gazing up at the leafy heights. His sorcerer trudged nervously behind him.

As ancient as the ground itself, the ivory birch trees stood in a perfect ring. Each trunk was as broad as a man's body. Their airy limbs swept up and intertwined at a central point above the grove, forming a foliate dome. Lodged in the crook of each tree was a copper urn, stained with ripples of bluish-green by the passage of time. Slow growth had partially subsumed some of the urns into the bodies of the trees, enveloping them in living wooden cocoons.

"And so I am come to the final resting place of Damon and his fathers," declared Ademar. "The council chamber of the wise and glorious dead! Tell me, do the hearts of Arbethia's kings beat steadfastly for the motherland? Or do they grow weary of this world?"

A wind stirred the leaves. Gradually, the wind grew into hushed, sibilant whispers, the murmuring of countless voices. Their words were just beyond comprehension.

Ademar placed a hand on a tree trunk. He could feel a pulse emanating from beneath the bark.

"Are you ready, mage?" asked Ademar.

"Y-yes, sire," the sorcerer replied. "I have the vessel, the herbs, the wand, and the, um... the..." He gulped.

"The knife."

"Very good," said Ademar. He stood in the center of the grove and threw off his cloak. Next, he stripped off his shirt. He spread his arms wide and breathed in deeply. At last, he declared, "You may begin."

When Ademar returned to his chambers early the next morning, Queen Apraksha woke to the slow tread of his feet upon the floorboards. Nestled beneath the bedclothes, she feigned sleep, peeking through half-closed eyes. Her husband looked tired, but content. He was a little pale. The shadow of exhaustion ringed his eyes, and a touch of blood stained his tunic. As he undressed for bed, Apraksha noticed that his chest, though clean as one newly-bathed, was marred by a single faint, slim scar.

One bright morning, Ademar stood atop the palace walls, surveying the splendor that surrounded him. Arbethia's capitol was a forest of gold-capped wooden towers, each spire proudly adorned with banners flown taut in the wind. Small towns and villages dotted the undulating hills and valleys below. Beyond lay the kingdom's breadbasket, the Black Steppes. And then there were the mountains, the coast, and other lands besides, all the former charges of the late princes. Now, they belonged only to Ademar. All of it was his.

All, except…

"Far north," he said to himself. "The vast Wildwood, realm of dreams, dominion of the White Stag! Yes, for it is the Stag who commands the budding and turning of leaves, who knows the language of all beasts, who judges when the hunter may capture his prey and when he must return home empty-handed!" His brow burned with indignation. "Ever has man been denied a share in the Wildwood. Not a solitary tree may he call his own—not even the Grove of Kings. It all belongs, in the end, to the White Stag. Our monarchs are merely its stewards. If I could but take charge of the Wildwood, Arbethia would be the mightiest nation on earth. I would be ruler of two realms: one of men, and one of beasts."

That very day, Ademar assembled a hunting party to venture deep into the Wildwood.

Once inside the ancient forest, Ademar's knights and servants caught only small game: martens, foxes, fowl. All the while, Ademar himself made no attempt to slay any animal. He carried but a single arrow in his quiver.

Day plunged into dusk. The green shelter of the Wildwood thickened into damp shadowy tangles of black-bearded spruce. The heavy cloister of branches blocked out the sun.

"Your majesty," a servant implored, soft but urgent. "Begging your pardon, but as the hour is late, should we not make our way homeward? The Wildwood is no place to be stranded at night." His voice dropped to a whisper. "They say the Lord of the Forest is not a foe to face in the dark."

"Children's tales!" scoffed Ademar loudly. He waved his hand at the brooding enclosure of trees. "Why should I fear some faun who trips about the forest playing pranks on feckless trappers?"

"Sire!" sputtered the servant. "It is no laughing matter. To insult him is to all but summon his wrath!"

"Oh, but I should like to witness this wrath!" said Ademar. "Wait, I know! I shall stand stock-still and pretend I am a tree. Then he may *graze* upon me to death!" Ademar roared with laughter. "But perhaps he is too busy to show his cowardly face. He is not so much a lord as a harried nursemaid to the beasts of the wood."

Ademar chuckled some more. His men fell grave and silent. Not a leaf stirred in the forest.

A low pounding arose in the distance—deep, terrible, insistent. The ground began to throb beneath their feet. Every leaf and needle quivered with dread.

Then a force like a driving whirlwind barreled towards

them. Tree trunks cracked and fell to the ground. Men cried in alarm and scrambled for cover into the darkest thickets. The horses whinnied with fright and almost trampled their masters.

Ademar held his ground. Calmly, he withdrew the Golden Arrow from his quiver.

A towering whiteness materialized before them. Swiftly, it took the shape of some bestial form that was horrible to behold. Its pelt was a moonlit blizzard. Its eyes were red as coals, and its antlers were thorny branches of bone. The being's presence filled the grove. It stamped a hoof, and the hole it gouged into the earth could have made a grave for two men. Steam from its nostrils blotted out the last scraps of daylight visible through the trees. The creature's powerful muscles rippled up and down. It leaned onto its haunches and prepared to charge.

Wasting not a moment, Ademar nocked the Golden Arrow into his bow. He released it with an air-splitting snap.

The arrow struck the White Stag in the throat. The beast bellowed in agony. Thick blood poured down its heaving shoulders and soaked the forest floor. The Stag collapsed to the ground. The impact of its fall rattled men's teeth and fractured their ribs.

The dust had not even settled before the Golden

Arrow sprang from the corpse's neck. It landed neatly in Ademar's quiver. His knights and servants lay curled upon the ground, mute and mad with terror.

Ademar looked up and waved a hand at the treetops. The branches parted, and the first stars of evening shone dimly upon his smiling face.

"Gentlemen, you may rise now," said Ademar. "Let us make for home. I promise our journey will be a peaceful one, now that I am Lord of the Forest."

In the months that followed, Ademar spent more time than ever in the Wildwood. Leaves turned spring-green or autumn-red a dozen times a day, depending on his mood. With his retinue at his side, he explored the forest day and night. He hunted whatever and whenever he pleased. The creatures were drawn to him, their animal wits dulled to a mindless stupor. They seemed unwilling to struggle or flee. Even the trees leaned aside to let the huntsmen's horses gallop wherever fancy took them. And yet, now that the hunt was so easy, it was becoming harder and harder to find the sport in it.

Ademar returned home from the Wildwood one day covered in a sheen of sweat and grime. He summoned his servants to draw him a bath. A basin was brought to his bedchamber. Ademar eased into the basin, allowing the hot water to soothe his tired muscles. As he watched the white steam coiling off the water's surface, a thought rippled across his mind.

"What good is it to be lord of so much land, when the Land Beneath the Waves is beyond my grasp?" He swept his hand back and forth through the water, making tiny currents in the bath. "The sea brims with untold riches. But so long as it belongs to the great Red Pike, it is a locked coffer of gold, a field lying fallow. I will not be content without it!"

Right then and there, he summoned for a crew of the hardiest sailors and keenest navigators. They would take the royal galleon out upon the heaving western seas. "Have them assembled and ready to depart for the coast," exclaimed Ademar, "before my bath grows cold!"

Lightning shattered the black horizon. Waves lashed the ship mercilessly. Torrents of rain pummeled the crew as the sky above them deepened to the color of wet slate. It was an uncanny false nighttime that devoured midday.

"Sire!" pleaded the ship's captain. "This is folly! We must make for port ere the storm swallows us whole!"

Ademar paid the captain no heed. He stood at the prow, one hand firmly grasping the rail, the other shielding his face. His eyes swept the horizon for signs of his quarry. Stoic as a figurehead, he sliced through the wet, wild air with his steely gaze.

And then, he saw it.

A flicker of scarlet peeked through the churning black water. Then it disappeared as quickly as it had emerged.

"That way!" bellowed Ademar. He pointed southwest. "Steer the ship *that way*!"

"But we cannot!" moaned the captain. "It is impossible!"

"Oh, there are things that seem impossible now, captain. But soon, nothing upon or below the sea will be beyond reach! Bring the bait above deck."

"But sire—"

"Bring it up!"

The crew hauled up an enormous iron cauldron from below decks. It was seven arm-spans around and filled to the brim with pure white pearls.

"Tip it into the sea!" cried Ademar. "All of it!"

The crew obeyed. The shimmering hoard of pearls cascaded over the ship's starboard side.

With a crack, a blaze of lightning split the mainsail mast in two. Ropes snapped. Hoarse shouts filled the air as the mast plunged into the sea. The boat pitched wildly to one side. Three men fell overboard. Those who remained clung desperately to any piece of wood, metal, or rope still attached to the ship.

Only Ademar, standing upright and clutching the railing, gave the chaos no mind. His eyes were fixed upon the churning sea. The black water bubbled and boiled in a whirl of white pearls and ruby scales.

Then the waves burst in a frenzy of foam. A serpentine, blood-red column muscled its way up from the depths. It snapped at the air, its teeth a thousand glittering needles crammed into a harpoon-like jaw. Its eyes were windows into the darkest caverns of the deepest seas.

Ademar released his grip on the railing just long enough to pull back a bowstring. He sent the Golden Arrow straight into the belly of the Red Pike.

The monstrous fish writhed and shuddered. It coiled and flailed. It stirred the tempestuous seas round and round until a whirlpool took shape. The ship was being drawn down into the swirling abyss. Men sobbed out prayers, only to have them torn from their lips by the fierce gale. Then, just when it seemed the ship was ready to plunge them all into oblivion, the Red Pike jumped up and froze rigid in mid-air. It fell against the water's surface with a deafening smack. Its body drifted down in a hiss of bubbles until an undercurrent dragged it forever out of sight of living men.

At once, the waves turned glassy and calm. The ship tipped upright. The wind and rain did not cease, but the sea seemed strangely unaffected by it.

A bolt of bright gold shot up from the still water and rested in Ademar's waiting quiver.

"Let us now make for port, gentlemen," said Ademar. "The sky may be cruel, but the sea has given up the fight. It knows who its master is."

At home in his palace, Ademar lay sick for seven days. The wind and rain had chilled him to the marrow. Strange dreams haunted his fever-wracked brain.

...the furious skeleton of the White Stag, impaling Ademar on sharp antlers...

...a red fog, the ghost of the Pike, wrapping its lithe body around Ademar and biting off his head...

...his head, sinking to the bottom of the sea, his eyes turning into pearls...

Vision after fearful vision passed through his mind. Then, gradually, all that remained were endless grey dreams of wind and rain. Exhale after icy exhale. The dream-wind forced Ademar to lie flat upon the ground while a shadowy bird of prey slashed and pecked at his chest. The bird was seeking a heart to feast upon. Yet it found nothing inside Ademar but an empty, black hollow.

...high above the storm clouds, a vast field of sunlit blue skies spread into infinity... its warmth and light were just out of reach...

On the dawning of the eighth day, Ademar awoke. He threw off his blankets as though they were on fire. In a wild fury, he exclaimed, "What use is it to be master of land and sea? What use, when the sky rules above both? The Black Falcon—he who is lord of every feathered thing in the air, he whose wings change the paths of the wind, whose cry calls rain from the heavens—he has been king of the skies long enough. It is time I seized the sky from his talons. I will not be denied what I desire."

The wind was cold, hard, and dry out on the high cliffs of southeastern Arbethia. It nipped at Ademar's cloak and pulled at his hair. Dust and sand flew into his eyes. Not once did he cower from the gusts, though his servants could hardly walk upright against the relentless blast. This was the most forsaken corner of the kingdom.

"How much higher must we go?" shouted Queen Apraksha above the roar of the wind. She pulled her cowl tight over her head.

"Not much longer, my nightingale," crooned Ademar. He grinned, but did not look back at her.

Very soon they came upon an enormous nest of

withered vines and branches. Six horses could have lain in it comfortably. The bones of deer and cattle were strewn about the ground. In the center of the nest was an egg the size of a barrel. Its shell was of malachite, blue and green mottled with white.

"This is it!" cried Ademar. He grabbed Apraksha by the hand and led her beside the nest. He could hardly contain his anticipation. "Sweet Apraksha, honey-throated Apraksha! The time has come. Sing."

Reluctantly, the queen took down her hood. Closing her eyes, she drew a deep breath. A piercing note escaped her lips. It was so high, so sweet, it made the ear and the heart ache all at once. She sang long and loud. No amount of wind could silence her.

A hairline crack formed in the stone shell of the egg. Ademar was overcome with delight. Queen Apraksha's singing had caused the desired effect.

A cry rent the air that rivaled Apraksha's voice. Dark whirlwinds swirled above the cliff. Fragments of shadow spiraled from every direction. The shadows became feathers, and the feathers coalesced into a vast winged form with desolate white eyes. Its talons were sharper than the crescent moon. Its bright beak could cut in half the very note that hung on the air.

The Black Falcon shrieked again and swept

downward. It grabbed the queen by her yellow braid and hoisted her into the sky. Apraksha screamed for her life, kicking and thrashing at the air. Servants stared in horror, but their limbs felt numb and heavy, their sight clouded and confused. As in all things, their will was subject to Ademar's will. They stood by and watched, powerless.

From under his cloak, Ademar produced a bow and the Golden Arrow. In a flash, the arrow was launched. It struck the Black Falcon squarely in the eye.

The Falcon let out a rasping wail that echoed up and down every mountain. It relinquished Apraksha from its talons. The queen fell to the ground and landed with a sickening crack. She lay there limp as a rag doll.

The Falcon spun and jerked round in the air. Its inky black feathers turned translucent. Then, like a ghostly vapor, it disintegrated into a thousand ragged shadows and scattered in every direction.

"Sire, the queen!" a servant wept. "She is... she is dead!"

Ademar caught the Golden Arrow in his quiver. "There is no need to shout," he said flatly. "Can you not hear? The wind has calmed down."

Ademar had achieved what no king before him had ever done: he was now ruler of land, sea, and sky. His body surged with power. It filled his brain, his lungs, and his bones with a suffusion of light. Some days, the power burned so bright and fierce within him, he feared his skin might split from the heat. He took to stalking about the palace with little or no clothes on, sweating profusely. Sometimes he thought the light spilled from his mouth when he spoke. Perhaps it did; for now man and beast, cloud and tree, all did as he commanded without hesitation.

And yet there was still something missing— something in the design of the world which eluded Ademar. He could not look this thing in the face, yet he saw it all around him. He could not hold it in his hand, yet its touch was an everyday presence. Ademar could gaze upon cities and forests and mountains and seas and call them his own, yet this one thing could look upon all of creation and know that it was still the greater master.

"The Sun," hissed Ademar. His voice seethed with venom. He stood atop the palace roof, casting clouds across the sky to block out the rays of daylight. "It looks down upon me, down upon the glory and majesty I have made of Arbethia. And all it can do is mock me! I will not be so maligned. I will not be made to bow before anyone." He paced back and forth across the roof. "Nine times, nine times," he muttered under his breath. "Nine times, ten times? Ten times, and then what? It cannot be tarnished, cannot be *sundered*, cannot, cannot... But nine times, ten times, and then... and then..." He paused. An idea entered his heated brain.

"But I *will* be master!" he cried. "And no price shall I pay! For how can the ferryman collect his toll, when the passenger has drowned him in the river?" He laughed shrilly. "Mage!" he called through the smoke hole in the roof. "Mage, are you down there? Of course you are, mage. Don't think I can't tell when you're eavesdropping on me. I can hear the rustling of those ridiculous robes of yours. Answer me, mage!"

There was a moment of silence. Then, "...yes, sire."

"Mage, go and fetch the locked chest from under my bed. Bring it up here."

"Yes, sire."

The chest was hauled up to the roof by a rope. Ademar took from around his neck a small brass key on a silver chain and unlocked the chest. Inside it was the Golden Arrow, along with a simple wooden bow.

"Mage," whispered Ademar, almost affectionately. He did not look at the sorcerer, but studied the arrow with intense interest. "Mage, have you ever been inside a smithy?"

"Yes, my lord, once or twice," said the sorcerer. He

did not even bother to be puzzled. There was little the king did or said that made sense anymore.

"And have you ever seen a smith work in gold?"

"I cannot say I have, sire. But I once had a great-uncle who was goldsmith to King Damon, long ago."

"And do you know how it is they change the shape of gold, mage? How they turn a mere lump of raw metal into a handful of coins, a queen's bracelet, or a king's crown?"

"Well, by melting it down, of course. And hammering it into shape after that."

"By melting it down..." Ademar repeated. "But what if there is no hammer?"

"I... I don't know, my lord. I suppose it cools into whatever form it takes, whatever shape it falls into. It becomes merely... another lump."

Ademar grinned, ecstatic. "Precisely."

He reached for the bow and nocked the Golden Arrow. The bowstring groaned as he pulled it back tightly.

"My lord, what are you doing...?"

"Oh mage," chuckled Ademar, staring straight into the sun. His eyes burned, but the pain was only a challenge to be met and answered. "Mage, you will see. Everyone will see. I cannot miss. *It* cannot miss! With this tenth strike, everything the sun's light touches will be *mine*. All things above and below heaven will be under my rule! And the Golden Arrow will be no better than a rock. That is, if it does not first boil to vapor in its final victim."

With a sound like a breaking harp string, he launched the Golden Arrow skyward.

"Mage," said Ademar placidly, "be so good as to summon my minstrels and cupbearers to join us here on the roof. It is a fine and pleasant day. I desire music and wine as we wait for the sun to die."

The rooftop feast carried on for a fortnight. Ademar was in the highest of spirits. Each day he called more and more members of the court to join him. He even invited petty merchants and common beggars of the streets to climb up ropes and ladders and sit beside his knights and noblewomen. Ademar's bottomless hospitality made the roof sag under the weight of the party. But as long as the wine flowed freely, the festivities continued. Few understood what the king was celebrating. Most knew it was better not to ask.

One day, a little pageboy was sitting on the roof nibbling a loaf of bread. He spoke not a peep as the party carried on. His eyes wandered to the horizon. All of a sudden, he stopped mid-chew. "Look!" he squeaked timidly. He tugged the sorcerer's sleeve. "Look, there is a fire! A fire at a farm on the hill!"

"Why, so there is," said the sorcerer, peering in the same direction. He was the only one who heard the boy. "It must have just caught fire a moment ago... And over there too!" He pointed to another site further south. "And—and there! There are at least half a dozen farmhouses on fire!"

"Then the farmers ought to take better care of their homes," scoffed Ademar through a mouthful of juicy apple. He dined languidly on a plate of fruit, enjoying the spectacle of a troupe of lady dancers. Their lively footwork made the roof creak and groan.

At that moment, a tuft of roof thatching ignited. The celebrants shrieked and bounded off their cushions. A servant tried to smother the fire with a blanket.

A drop of brightness fell from the sky. More thatching caught on fire. Another drop fell, and another, each bigger than the last. Soon, half the roof was ablaze. The guests dispersed in terror. Some jumped down the smoke hole, others off the roof into the courtyard below.

"Mage, what is happening?" asked Ademar.

"My lord, it is raining fire!" cried the sorcerer. "On the palace, on the city, everywhere! Come, we must get down off the roof!"

"Why is it raining fire? Mage, *why is this happening*?"

More blazes sprang up. The sky grew dimmer.

"Sire, the Sun... it is... bleeding."

Ademar announced that as Lord of the Skies, he would make it rain to quench the fiery downpour. But the sun's blood proved too strong. The rain burned to mist before it even reached the ground.

So Ademar declared that as Lord of the Seas, he would summon the oceans to flood the land and douse the fires.

"But sire," said the sorcerer, "all will drown!"

So Ademar ordered a thousand stout warriors, a thousand woodsmen, and a thousand carpenters to fell a thousand trees in the great northern Wildwood. They would build a boat to float the palace to safety. Peasants and townsmen would have to find their own higher ground.

"Mage, you will go with the woodcutters. There is one tree in the Wildwood they must *not* use until I have split it myself. You know which tree I speak of. Fell it with your own hands, and guard it with your life until it is delivered to me."

So a thousand trees were felled. All but one were hewn into beams and planks and masts. The palace was lifted from its very foundations, and a ship of unprecedented size and majesty was built around it. Ademar ordered a hundred of the most virtuous ladies in the kingdom to weave a hundred sails out of spider's silk. Fifty of the fairest-haired maidens were ordered to cut off their golden braids to make ropes for the sails.

All the while, fire rained down upon the world. The sun grew dimmer as its life drained away.

With the last nail driven into the last plank of wood, and the last rope of hair raising the final silken sail, Ademar called forth the seas. He called the water to rise up from its sleep and cover the dry, burning land. A great deluge engulfed the earth. It filled every valley and flooded every plain. Only boats and the bare mountaintops were spared. The palace ship rose with the water level. Then with a heaving groan, it launched out upon the waves. Ademar used one hand to summon a wind to guide the sails; in his other hand he clutched a small copper urn.

Many of the ship's planks were burned or scorched in the journey. It was all the servants could do to vigilantly quench the outbreaks of flame. On the ninth day of sailing, the ship began to leak. On the tenth day, it was sinking.

"My lord, we will drown!" despaired the sorcerer. "What will you do?"

"I am still lord of all things under the sun!" proclaimed Ademar. "At least, what remains of it. I shall summon aid." He raised his hand up to the sky.

A lamentation of massive, snowy white swans flocked towards the sinking ship. Ademar stretched out his arm to them, pleading.

"Noble swans!" he cried. "You, who are the frost upon the lake sedge, the foam upon every wave, the snowcaps of the sea. Hear me now: I command you! Bear us upon your backs, and fly us to higher ground."

In a rush of downy wings, the swans rose from the water and landed on the sinking palace deck. Ademar took hold of the biggest, strongest-looking swan and mounted its back. "Take us unto the eastern cliffs!" he shouted.

The giant swan beat its powerful wings and lifted into the sky.

Ademar clung tightly to the swan's body with his right arm. With his left, he held the copper vessel close to his breast. Glancing behind him, he could see the other escapees following on swan-back at a distance. Below him was his kingdom. It was a charred, steaming wreckage of the glory Arbethia had been mere days before.

The swan trumpeted something in its own tongue.

Ademar, as Lord of the Skies, understood every word. "The sky grows dimmer, my king!" the swan cried. "Soon, darkness will be upon us. I fear I may not find the place you seek."

"Just keep flying!" shouted Ademar. "We will reach it soon enough."

After an hour, the swan cried again, "The sky grows dimmer yet, my king! Here, the fire rains thickest. I cannot fly much longer."

"Do not slow down!" said Ademar.

Another hour passed, and suddenly the swan jerked to one side, mid-flight. It screeched in pain. "My eyes, my eyes! A drop of fire has fallen into my eyes. I am blinded! Farewell, King Ademar. I can fly no more."

"But we are almost there! There is a high cliff, just beyond—"

But it was too late. The swan twisted about violently. Ademar lost his grip and pitched headlong through the air. The bird dropped like a stone through a mass of clouds, and was gone.

Ademar plummeted through the sky. Hot tears streamed from his eyes, blowing skywards like rain in reverse. The air around him was bitter, empty, and dark. Surely this was the end for him. He felt cold, so very cold. He fell down, down, down.

And then he landed. He was lying in something cushioned, but prickly. Ademar hauled his bruised and bleeding self up and looked around. He knew this place! He had fallen into the Black Falcon's nest! Even the cracked egg was still there. A thrill of joy ran through him. What tremendous luck!

But where was the copper vessel? Ademar scrambled out of the nest. The broken remains of the urn were scattered across the hard ground. Then he saw it. Ademar breathed a sigh of relief. There was his heart: red and glistening as the day it was plucked from his chest. It lay beating in the sand, whole and unharmed.

Ademar gathered up his heart and wiped it clean. He would keep it safe under a ledge or a cave until the sun had bled dry. Then he would make the waters recede, and seek out what might remain of civilization.

Ademar's ears pricked up. There was a curious whistling noise coming from afar. He looked about, but saw nothing. He shrugged off the feeling of dread and cradled his heart close to him. Then he turned to go seek shelter.

The whistling grew louder. Then it grew lower, and nearer, and louder still, until—

Thud.

Something landed in Ademar's hands. He shrieked. The bones of his hands were shattered. Bewildered with pain, he looked down. Lodged in the center of his heart was a lump of pure, bright, solid gold.

Ademar stared, transfixed. Then he watched with

horror as his heart burned to ash in his hands. The organ that was once the seat of his soul now dispersed into the sky as so much dust upon the wind.

Ademar felt the last of the heat of power leave his body.

The sun ceased its bleeding. Elsewhere, floods withdrew. Now, the world belonged to itself again.

Light would return to the earth in time. But for Ademar, eternal night was upon him.

ABOUT THE AUTHOR

Author, musician, and artist **Samantha Gillogly** began reading fairy stories at such a young age that she hasn't quite figured out how to stop.

Her essay "Apiarian Days," which chronicles her experience placing 16th in the 2001 Scripps Howard National Spelling Bee, was featured in the 2007 Hudson Street Press anthology, *Red: The Next Generation of American Writers—Teenage Girls—On What Fires Up Their Lives Today.* The essay was later reprinted in textbooks for Pearson and the U.S. State Department.

Samantha currently resides in the northeastern U.S.

The Golden Arrow and Other Tales is her first book of fiction.

To learn more, visit:
www.SamanthaGillogly.com

or drop the author a line at:
Samantha@samanthagillogly.com

www.ingramcontent.com/pod-product-compliance
Lightning Source LLC
Chambersburg PA
CBHW030556130626
46552CB00006B/2570